CAMPER OF THE WEEK

STORY AND PICTURES BY

AMY SCHWARTZ

ORCHARD BOOKS   NEW YORK

Orchard Books, A division of Franklin Watts, Inc.
387 Park Avenue South, New York, NY 10016

Manufactured in the United States of America. Printed by General Offset Company, Inc.
Bound by Horowitz/Rae. Book design by Mina Greenstein.
The text of this book is set in 16 point Schneidler. The illustrations are pen-and-ink with
watercolor wash and pencil, reproduced in full color.   10 9 8 7 6 5 4 3 2 1

Library of Congress Cataloging-in-Publication Data
Schwartz, Amy. Camper of the week : story and pictures / by Amy Schwartz.   p.   cm.
Summary: Although Rosie, a model camper, does not participate in her friends' prank and is not
caught and disciplined, she decides to join her friends in the punishment because she knows she
helped them.
ISBN 0-531-05942-1.   ISBN 0-531-08542-2
[1. Camps—Ficton.   2. Behavior—Fiction.   3. Friendship—Fiction.]   I. Title.
PZ7.S406Cam 1991   [E]—dc20   90-23033

MT(54)

MAY - - 1992

FOR MY PARENTS

A hush fell over the Camp Wicky-Wack campers as Big John slowly opened the birchbark folder.

Rosie clutched her hands in tight little fists.

The twins, Dawn and Eve, each put a warm hand on each of Rosie's knees.

"And the Camp Wicky-Wack Camper of the Week," read Big John, "is…

"Rosie Matthews from Badger Cabin."

"Hurray!" the twins cheered.

A spitball hit the back of Rosie's head.

"Cut it out, Bernice!" snarled Rosie's buddy Rhonda.

"Rosie Matthews is courteous and considerate," Big John continued over the campers' applause as Rosie walked to the front of the mess hall to receive her burl plaque. "Rosie Matthews obeys all Camp Wicky-Wack rules. Rosie Matthews is a credit to her fellow Badgers."

Rosie cradled the burl to her chest as she trailed the Badgers back to the cabin under the setting sun.

She carefully placed her award under her pillow. Then she changed into her robe and go-aheads and took her toiletry bag to the girls' bathroom to wash up for bed.

Rhonda and the twins were there, brushing each other's hair.

"Yo, Rosie! First in your pj's as always!" Rhonda greeted her.

"Congratulations, Camper of the Week," Dawn said. "I knew you'd get it. You are so good. You never get in trouble!"

"Yes, I do," Rosie said, "all the time." *No,* she thought to herself. *Never. I never, ever get in trouble.*

"Well," Eve said, "if you want to, you can get in trouble with us." She pointed to the sink. Three shiny minnows were lying there, side by side.

"A few fish for Bernice's bed." Rhonda giggled. "Want to help us give that bully a surprise? I can't believe she hit you with that spitball."

Rosie stepped back. "Oh...no...I couldn't. I'm...I'm allergic to fish."

"You mean allergic to trouble." Rhonda laughed. "That's okay, Rosie." The girls gathered up their things. "But, if you change your mind, meet us at Bernice's bed at eight-thirty. She has KP tonight. See you later."

Rosie brushed her teeth and gargled twice. It was cold and a little spooky in the girls' bathroom. She brushed her hair one hundred times.

Rosie watched a centipede make its way down a drainpipe. She rubbed the back of her head where Bernice's spitball had hit. Then she thought of Bernice's bare feet finding the three minnows between the sheets, and laughed.

"I'd still be a courteous camper if all I did was watch," Rosie told the centipede. She checked the time. She had three minutes. Rosie zipped up her toiletry bag and hurried outside.

"Well, well, if it isn't Miss Goody Two Shoes, all ready for bed!"

Rosie froze in her tracks. It was Bernice heading back to the cabin. *She'll catch Rhonda and the twins for sure!*

"Help!" Rosie threw her toiletry bag in the air and fell down. "Help me, Bernice! It's my knee!"

Bernice laughed. "Some Camper of the Week!"

Rosie moaned and groaned. Bernice kept laughing. A moment later Rosie saw three figures slip from the cabin. She sat up.

"I'm okay," she said to Bernice. "It's all better now."

A few minutes after lights out, a shriek rang out from the Badger Cabin.

At breakfast the next morning, Big John looked over the Wicky-Wack mess hall. "I'd like to see the McKenzie twins and Rhonda Rabinowitz in my office. Pronto."

Rosie's stomach flip-flopped. She saw Bernice in the corner of the hall, with a triumphant smirk on her face.

"What'll he do to us?" whispered Dawn.

"We've gotta stick together!" Eve said.

"So long, Rosie," Rhonda said. "Lucky for you that you're so good."

Rosie watched her three friends file out after Big John. She was all alone at the long table.

During basket weaving, Rhonda filled Rosie in.
"Bernice figured out it was us, so we had to confess.
Big John said we can't go to the Ghost Story Powwow
tomorrow night."

Rosie gasped. The powwow was the most exciting
event at Camp Wicky-Wack.

"Hey, man, it's okay," Rhonda said. "We'll have our
own powwow. Don't worry about us."

Rosie watched Rhonda and the twins huddled together,
whispering and giggling as they wove their baskets.

During archery, Bobby Jones pulled Rosie's ponytail. "Heard about those girls?" he said. "Three minnows! They're really something!"

"It's about time someone gave that bully a taste of her own medicine," Sherman Bronstein piped in.

And at late afternoon swim, the kids on the raft could talk of nothing else.

At supper Rosie sat down with her friends.

"So what if we got caught," Dawn was saying. "It was worth it! Those fish sure made Bernice scream!"

"We're lucky she didn't catch us putting them in her bed," Rhonda chimed in.

"Really lucky," said Eve. "Bernice got out of KP early that night, but came back to the cabin too late to catch us anyway." Eve shook her head. "Isn't that something, Rosie?"

Rosie dragged her fork through her mashed potatoes so it made little tracks.

"Well, we've gotta find moss for our dioramas," Dawn said. "Catch you later, Rosie."

Rhonda and the twins ran out of the door. Rosie decided to go check her Camper of the Week award.

The burl was still there in the empty cabin. Rosie changed into her robe and go-aheads. She put the burl under her arm and went out to the bathroom to brush her teeth. She watched the centipede on the drainpipe as she brushed her hair one hundred times.

"I am the Camper of the Week," she told her reflection in the mirror. "I obey all Camp Wicky-Wack rules." The centipede continued down the pipe. "Most of the time."

Rosie put the burl in her toiletry bag and slowly walked back to the cabin.

At Friday morning forestry Rosie couldn't concentrate on tree rings, and during the picnic lunch she didn't feel very hungry. She looked up and saw Big John watching her. He picked up his sandwich and came and sat next to her. Rosie watched him eat.

"Why so glum, Camper of the Week? Want a pickle?"

Rosie nodded. She watched a huge piece of cake disappear into Big John's mouth. She took a bite of her pickle and chewed it very carefully.

Then she picked up a twig and drew a circle in the dirt. "If a person breaks a Camp Wicky-Wack rule," Rosie said in a small voice, "is that person still a credit to her cabin?"

"Well, it all depends," Big John said.

Rosie drew a wavy line around the circle. She looked over at her three pals. She was sure they were planning their powwow. "If a person's friends get caught doing something, and that person isn't caught, but maybe should have been, wouldn't that person feel kind of lonely?"

"Well, Rosie, yes, I could see that a person might feel that way." Big John brushed some crumbs from his beard. He stood up. "See you at the powwow tonight?"

"I guess so," Rosie replied.

After dinner that night the Badgers hurried back to their cabin to get ready for the Ghost Story Powwow. Big John rang the camp gong and called out, "Five minutes!"

All the Badgers ran to the campfire. Except for Rhonda and the twins.

And Rosie.

"I decided to stay here with you," she said. "Because
I helped with the fish. I was the one who made Bernice late."

"Yo, Rosie!" Rhonda cried. "Thanks!"

"You old troublemaker!" Eve laughed. "I knew you had
it in you!"

The Camper of the Week joined her three buddies.
And, in the corner of the Badger Cabin, the four friends
told each other ghost stories until their toes curled.

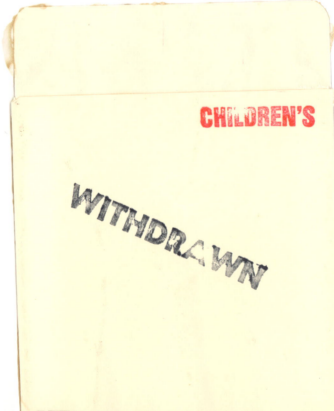